Captain Midnight
and the Granny Bag

BUNCH OF BADDIES

THE CACTUS BOYS

CAPTAIN MIDNIGHT AND
THE GRANNY BAG

GALACTACUS THE AWESOME

THE VOYAGE OF
THE PURPLE PRAWN

Captain Midnight
and the Granny Bag

Andrew Matthews

Illustrated by
André Amstutz

ORCHARD BOOKS

for Jess, with love
A.M.

ORCHARD BOOKS
96 Leonard Street, London EC2A 4RH
Orchard Books Australia
14 Mars Road, Lane Cove, NSW 2066
ISBN 1 85213 778 9 Hardback
ISBN 1 85213 875 0 Paperback
First published in Great Britain 1994
First paperback publication 1996
Text © Andrew Matthews 1994
Illustrations © André Amstutz 1994
The right of Andrew Matthews to be identified as the Author
and André Amstutz as the Illustrator of this Work
has been asserted by them in accordance with
the Copyright, Designs and Patents Act, 1988.
A CIP catalogue record for this book is available
from the British Library.
Printed in Great Britain.

CONTENTS

1. On Hangman's Heath 7

2. The Withered Weasel 22

3. Deadly Secrets 36

4. Hangman's Heath Again ..53

1

ON HANGMAN'S HEATH

*I*T was a clear night. The full moon shone down on a mail coach as it rocked and rattled along the road, which picked and twisted its way across a wide stretch of wild heathland.

In his seat on top of the coach, the driver cracked his whip, while beside him the

guard clutched grimly at a blunderbuss.

" 'Angman's 'Eath!" the guard said above the clattering of the horses' hoofs. "I never 'ave liked this place!"

"Go on with you!" said the driver. "In two hours' time the mail will be on board the boat from Dover to Boulogne and we'll be toastin' our toes in the snug of The Parrot and Posset."

"I can't 'elp it!" shuddered the guard.
"On 'Angman's 'Eath there's too many
gorse bushes and oak trees for an 'ighwayman to 'ide be'ind!"

"You're all tensed up, that's your trouble,"
said the driver. "You want to relax a bit,
before your imagination starts playin'
tricks on you!"

"What tricks?" the guard frowned.

"Well, if you ain't careful, you might start seein' things," the driver said. "I mean, see that oak tree up ahead – the one with the thick shadow under it? Well if I was to let my imagination run away with me, I might think that shadow looked like a man in a cocked-'at and cloak, mounted on a fine stallion!"

As soon as the driver had finished speaking, the shadow under the tree moved out into the moonlight in the middle of the road. It was a man in a cocked-hat and cloak, mounted on a fine stallion. The man pulled a pair of pistols from his saddle-holsters.

"Stand and deliver!" he cried.

His voice rang out like a hammer striking iron. The driver hauled on the reins and the coach came to a halt.

Now that they were closer, the driver and the guard could see that the highwayman was wearing a black mask that covered the top half of his face.

"Who the devil are you?" called out the guard.

"They call me Captain Midnight," the highwayman replied. "This is my trusty steed, Brown Bryan, and these are my trusty duelling-pistols. One is aimed straight at your heart and the other is aimed straight at yours, driver. One false move and I'll fill you full of lead!"

"Much obliged, I'm sure, guv!" the driver said nervously.

"What d'you want?" asked the guard.

"What do I want?" Captain Midnight repeated mockingly. "I want to rob the coach, of course. What did you think I wanted – a cosy chit-chat?"

"I'm sorry, but the answer's no," said the guard. "This is a Royal Mail coach, and in Royal Mail regulations it says it's my job to guard it with my blunderbuss. What right 'ave you got to stop this coach and steal anything that takes your fancy?"

"Watch this!" said Captain Midnight.

Without even turning his head to look, he pointed his left pistol over his right shoulder and fired it behind him. The bullet hit a milestone at the side of the road and bounced off it – YEEANG! – on to the

rim of one of the coach's wheels, bounced
off that – PEEYONG! – and knocked the
blunderbuss out of the guard's hands
before cutting through the reins.

"Fair enough," said the guard. "Anything
in particular that you had your eye on?"

"I like the look of that small, brass-bound box," said Captain Midnight, pointing with his smoking pistol. "If that box isn't stuffed with gold doubloons, I'll boil my boots in brandy! And there may be many a nifty knick-knack in that big sack over there. Fetch 'em both down for me, there's a good fellow!"

Five minutes later, Captain Midnight was speeding off across Hangman's Heath with the brass-bound box under his arm and the sack tied securely across Brown Bryan's back.

The driver and the guard began knotting the reins back together while the horses snorted and stamped.

"So, that was Captain Midnight!" mused the guard. "A cut above your ordinary ruffian, ain't 'e? 'E's what I'd call a true gentleman of the road."

"I reckon we could do all right out of this," said the driver. "If we tell our story

to the papers and lay it on a bit thick – we might make a quid or two."

"Blood and thunder!" cried the guard, clapping a hand to his forehead.

"What is it?" asked the driver.

"I didn't ask him for his autograph!" said the guard. "The wife and kids won't ever let me 'ear the end of it!"

2

THE WITHERED WEASEL

WHEN Captain Midnight was out of sight of the coach, he ripped off his mask with a careless laugh. "On, Brown Bryan!" he cried. "Carry me to the arms of Polly, my true love, with skin as soft as summer meadows and hair as black as a raven's wing!"

There was a lot more of this sort of thing, and Brown Bryan was glad that he didn't understand a word of it. He carried his master at a gallop, slowing to a steady trot when he reached the outskirts of the village of Much Littling.

"With eyelashes like humming-birds' tongues, and fingernails like sugared almonds, and – oh, we're here!"

Brown Bryan had stopped in the court-yard of an inn. Next to the inn stood a tall pole with a sign on top of it.

The inn was quiet and all its windows were dark.

"Ah!" sighed Captain Midnight. "My dearest is deep in the vale of slumber!"

He leapt down from the saddle and flit-
ted across the cobbled courtyard like a
cruising barn-owl. With the brass-bound
box still tucked under his arm, he shinned
up the pole, stepped on to a small, flat
roof and clambered up an ivy-covered wall
until he reached a window. He tapped

gently on the glass. "Polly?" he whispered. "Open the window! It is I, your secret love!"

The window swung open at once, clunking the highwayman on the head, and Polly's face appeared. She didn't look pleased. "What on earth d'you think you're up to, climbing the ivy at this time of night?" she snapped. "You haven't forgotten your front-door key again, have you?"

Captain Midnight blushed, "E-r-r...," and then gushed, "How could I remember anything except your beauty?"

"Oh, do give over!" groaned Polly. "Sometimes you're wetter than a newt's nostrils! I wish you'd get yourself a proper job instead of gallivanting about at all hours! Now be off with you and come back in the morning!"

"But I brought you this, my love!" said Captain Midnight, holding up the brass-bound box. "Freshly robbed from the Royal Mail coach!"

"What's in it?" Polly asked.

"Gold perhaps – or diamonds!" said Captain Midnight. "Let me climb in through your window, my treasure, and we can open it together."

"Only if you promise me that there won't be any soppy stuff!" Polly said sternly.

"Oh, very well, you heartless wench!" said Captain Midnight, swinging himself over the window-ledge.

After much muttering and fiddling, Polly managed to pick the lock of the brass-bound box and Captain Midnight looked on eagerly as she lifted the lid.

There were no diamonds in the box, or gold doubloons, either – just a piece of paper with a message written on it.

Dear Customer,
The Brass-Bound Box
Company takes great
pleasure in presenting
you with your free
surprise gift —
a brass-bound box!

"You great gawk!" exclaimed Polly. "Why didn't you look inside before you took it?"

"I was concentrating on my presentation," said Captain Midnight. "You should've seen the stylish way I held my pistols."

"Bother your pistols!" Polly said grumpily. "We'll never save enough money to be married at this rate! Let's face it, you're dashingly handsome and a crack shot, but when it comes to making money out of being a highwayman, you're a complete failure. Why don't you give it up and give me a hand running the inn?"

"Running the inn?" said Captain Midnight. "Where's the romance and poetry in running an inn? Where's the excitement and drama in – " He broke off suddenly. "Flog me with flamingo feathers, I forgot about the sack! I'll fetch it at once!"

He launched himself at the open window, but Polly caught him by the coat, dragged him back inside and made him use the stairs. He returned in a few minutes with the sack slung over his shoulder.

"Too light for gold bars or jewels," he told Polly. "Perhaps it's stuffed with newly printed banknotes!"

"Dream on!" said Polly.

The neck of the sack was tied shut with a piece of rope. The knot in the rope was stubborn, but Captain Midnight prised it loose at last. He was just about to open the sack and peer inside, when it twitched and a head popped up out of it. It was an old lady's head. Her hair was white and curly, her eyes were grey and sparkling and her smile was as sweet as sunbeams.

"Hello there!" she said cheerily. "Is this Bristol?"

3

DEADLY SECRETS

"WHO the deuce are you?" cried Captain Midnight. "And what are you doing in that bag?"

"I'm Granny Baskin," said the old lady. "I'm a poor widow woman, and now that my children have all left home, no one ever comes to visit me. I'm stuck in all day in my peasant cottage with nothing to do. Now I've decided to start a new life in the New World. I couldn't afford a ticket so I posted myself to Bristol so I could stow away on a ship. Am I in Bristol?"

"This is The Withered Weasel Inn at Much Littling," Polly said.

"Is it anywhere near Bristol?" Granny Baskin asked hopefully.

"Not really," Polly confessed.

"I knew I should never have trusted the Royal Mail!" grumbled Granny Baskin as she stepped out of the sack. "I shall just have to walk it."

"But Bristol is two hundred miles away!" spluttered Captain Midnight.

"I've no time to waste then," said Granny Baskin. She was walking towards the door when a thought struck her. "Just a

minute!" she frowned suspiciously. "Last
thing I remember before I dropped off to
sleep in my sack was being loaded on to a
mail coach. How did I get from there to
here?"

"I brought you," said Captain Midnight.

"And who are you?" Granny Baskin
demanded.

"Have a care!" Polly hissed. "Don't tell
her who you really are."

"I'm not going to!" Captain Midnight hissed back. "I'm going to tell her I'm Simon the stable-hand. What d'you take me for, a fool?"

"I just know what a big show-off you can be!" said Polly.

"Show-off?" shrieked Captain Midnight. "D'you think a bold highwayman like Captain Midnight would stoop to vanity?"

"Ooh!" exclaimed Granny Baskin. "A highwayman! Fancy!"

"Blue blazes!" cursed Captain Midnight. "She's found out my true identity. But fear not, sweet Polly, I'll never reveal that you are my secret love and I am yours!"

"Secret lovers? A-a-w, how romantic!" cooed Granny Baskin.

"You big lummock!" wailed Polly. "When will you learn to keep your big mouth shut?"

"Stap me vitals with a rusty rapier – Granny knows too much!" gasped Captain Midnight, drawing a pistol from his belt and pointing it at Granny Baskin. "We'll have to keep her quiet. One false move and I'll fill you full of lead, Granny."

"You're never going to shoot a poor old woman, are you?" said Polly.

"Oh, I suppose not!" said Captain Midnight. "We'll have to tie her up and keep her prisoner here."

"Righty-ho!" said Granny Baskin. "Anything's better than that old cottage of mine. D'you want to use the rope from my sack?"

"That's no good!" Polly scolded. "This is

only a small village. Somebody's bound to find out about her sooner or later."

"In that case," said Captain Midnight, "we'll have to make her give us a really, really, really big promise not to tell."

"I couldn't do that!" said Granny Baskin. "I won't make promises I can't keep and I'm a terrible gossip."

"Wouldn't you like us to take you back to your peasant cottage?" suggested Polly.

"No fear!" said Granny Baskin, folding her arms in a determined fashion. " I was lonely and miserable there and I'm not going back and that's that!"

"Then I can't think what to do!" sighed Polly.

"Tell you what," said Granny Baskin, "while you two are trying to make up your minds about what to do with me, why don't I make us all a nice cup of tea? Just point me at the kitchen!"

While Granny Baskin hummed and clattered about downstairs, Polly sat on the edge of her bed and twined a tress of her hair around one of her fingers. Captain Midnight paced up and down, running his hands through his hair and muttering to himself. Neither of them noticed the cooking smells coming up the stairs until Granny Baskin called out.

The table in the kitchen had been spread with a clean, white tablecloth and laid for three. In the centre of the table, coils of steam rose from the spout of a teapot and a plate of small pies. Granny Baskin bustled about with the sack tied round her like a pinafore.

"Tea's made. I did some baking in case
anybody was feeling peckish," she said.

Polly sat down, helped herself to a pie,
and began to eat.

Captain Midnight absent-mindedly
picked up a pie and bit into it. As soon as
he did so, his eyes lit up like lanterns.

"Gadzooks, but this is delicious!" he exclaimed.

"You're right!" Polly agreed. "However did you make them, Granny?"

"With a few leftovers I found," said Granny. "Nothing special."

"Yes it is!" said Captain Midnight. "The pastry is golden and meltingly light and the filling is super-scrummy! Why, if we served these pies at The Withered Weasel folk would travel for miles to eat them."

"No they wouldn't!" said Polly. "No one ever comes to Much Littling – that's why business is so bad. If only – "

THE ORIGINAL

Granny Pie

ONLY AT

The Withered Weasel

Polly stopped talking and went as still as a waxwork.

"Is she all right?" asked Granny Baskin.

"She's having an idea," Captain Midnight explained.

"Ooh!" said Granny Baskin. "Let's hope it's a good one!"

4

HANGMAN'S HEATH AGAIN

A FEW days later, in the dingy light before sunrise, a Royal Mail passenger coach bumped and swayed along the road that crossed a wild heath. Inside the coach, sleepy passengers napped, but in his seat outside the guard was wide awake and he cast uneasy glances at the countryside.

"'Angman's 'Eath again!" he said to the driver. "After what 'appened 'ere last time, this place fair gives me the wobblies!"

"Take it easy, mate!" said the driver. "Remember what they say – lightnin' never strikes in the same place twice!"

Just as the driver finished speaking, a man wearing a cocked-hat and a cloak rode his fine stallion out from the shadow of an oak tree into the middle of the road. He drew a pair of pistols from his saddle-holsters.

The horses whinnied and the iron rims on the wheels struck sparks from stones in the road as the coach screeched to a halt. The driver peered through the gloom.

"Well, bless my britches if it ain't our old pal Captain Midnight!" he cried. "'Ow are you, Cap?"

"Fine!" said Captain Midnight.

"And you've come to rob our coach again, I suppose, you audacious rogue!" chuckled the guard. He banged on the roof of the coach with the butt of his blunderbuss. "Oi, you lot!" he shouted. "Wake up and meet a real 'ighwayman!"

The door of the coach opened and the passengers bundled out, blinking like dozy owls. One of them, a plump man, wagged his finger at Captain Midnight.

"Don't think you're getting away with this, you viper-hearted varlet!" he blustered. "I'll have you know that I'm a Justice of the Peace!"

"Hold your tongue, Mr Wobbly Bottom!" said Captain Midnight. "One false move from you and I'll fill you full of – !"

"Hot pies and coffee!" shouted a voice. "Hot pasties and tea!"

From the shadows of the oak tree where Captain Midnight had hidden came a

small cart, pulled by a pretty white mare with blue ribbon-bows tied in her mane. The sides of the cart had been painted with the words "Highwayman Snacks" in brightly coloured letters. Polly sat in the driver's seat and on the back of the cart was Granny Baskin, with steaming urns of tea and coffee and a great pile of pies.

The passengers cheered and ran forward,
jostling to be first in the queue.

"Polly?" gasped Captain Midnight.
"Granny? What the devil d'you think
you're up to?"

"We're giving some refreshments to these
poor people!" said Polly. "They must be
starving hungry after spending hours
cramped up in that rickety old coach!
Come and help us!"

"What, me?" said Captain Midnight. "Become a tradesperson?"

"Oh, don't be such a snob!" said Granny. "Get down off that horse and give us a hand serving!"

Half an hour later the coach was on its way once more, filled with travellers who were sighing with contentment. Captain Midnight, Polly and Granny Baskin waved to them until the coach went out of sight.

"Weren't they smashing!" sighed Granny Baskin. "It's so nice to be doing something and out meeting lots of people again instead of being cooped up in a cottage!"

"And just look at this!" grinned Polly, holding up a bulging purse and jingling it under Captain Midnight's nose. "If we can keep this up, we'll be married in no time!"

"It wasn't too bad, I suppose," said Captain Midnight reluctantly.

"You were wonderful!" said Polly. "We make a great team - you hold up the coaches and then Granny and I can feed the passengers. You can put on a shooting display if you like. I'll throw buns up into the air and you can shoot holes through them to turn them into doughnuts!"

"Hmm!" said Captain Midnight, rubbing his chin. "That way I could keep up my reputation as a crack shot." He smiled at Polly and Granny Baskin. "Let's get back to The Withered Weasel and prepare for the afternoon coach!" he said briskly. "And make sure you put that money somewhere safe, Polly. After all, we don't want to get robbed on the way home, do we?"